For Monks Only
By Ralph-Michael Chiaia

One night when you lived in Brooklyn and

she lived in Kuala Lumpur, Liana Kim picked up her phone and then hung up on you before you could say a word. Her cell phone had caller ID. It could identify, from Malaysia, your phone plugged into your tiny kitchen wall. You dialed again. This time there was no answer. You called again. Everything stupid and scared inside you—all the jealousy like a line of dirty, lipstick-smeared shot glasses on a bar needing to be washed and all the paranoia like a brick bludgeoning the eye—grew a mushroom plant, a year-old yogurt, your mind was mold on a forgotten potato deep in the recesses of a refrigerator, the one that you smell even after you close the fridge door, a horrible, ugly muck that clogged your veins and lay you face down in the covers of the bed: Where was she? Who was she with? What was she doing? Why do you care so much? She picked up. The moldy potato was found! Ready to be thrown into the trash—you absolutely yearned to hear her voice, to be soothed—but, no, the phone froze! Was that possible? It wouldn't dial or change screens or anything. No volume. No keypad response. No Liana. Nothing. You detached the old battery, plugged the power cord into the socket, and called again tethered precariously to the wall like a jackass. This time it cut straight to voicemail (this was possible by pressing a button on the side of her phone). You called too many more times: 27. Pick up, damn you! She never picked up. You kneeled beside the bed, with your head on the bedspread and wept. You fought for her and now you were like muck.

White noise is so loud at thirty-five thousand feet and the air outside is cold: forty below zero. Elevated you know you still love her. It's not her, it's me, you think. You are the one whose soul has died—killed by routine, chopped up by monotony, sliced by comforts. If you had maintained her as well as your car, for example, she would have picked up the phone that night—and none of the unraveling of your relationship would have begun.

As the plane lands, the doubts resurface. That was probably all bullshit that you thought up there at thirty-five thousand feet.

You walk into the same Hong Kong airport where she was in that floral dress—or was it paisley?—months ago, when you were still elated all the time you were together. She was crying while she watched you pass through this same immigration. But now, back at sea level, you wonder if you still love her. In fact, you wonder if you ever loved her.

You were the one who had to leave her then. Maybe that meant something.

She was supposed to do a year long contract with Allen-Bradley, the company that built the computer controls to the Malaysian monorail in Kuala Lumpur. The monorail was running, although a chunk fell down onto a manicured grass lawn between two lanes of traffic recently, and she decided to stay on. Imagine a streamlined chunk of monorail in front of a Georgian house in a Muslim, Southeast Asian country. .

Now, 15,338.15 kilometers away from her and months later, you are traveling from a Brooklyn stoop to Southeast Asia. You are not going to Kuala Lumpur though. The reason not to go to her doorstep is that she hasn't spoken to you in a long time though she knew you had vacation time.

Instead of KL, you take the connecting flight into Manila's old, rickety airport. It's cramped, the décor is beige like a 1970s jacket with elbow pads worn by a guy with bushy sideburns, a moustache, and sunglasses that are bigger than his face. Now, three movies added to your mental library of Hollywood's reinvention of US history, you are 2,499.61 kilometers from her. You know now you want to recreate your relationship with her, relive it from another angle—somewhat like a bizzaro superman.

There are checkpoints for SARS and Avian Flu from which people out here have been dying. The checkpoints are empty although mariachis play boleros near the window behind it. After walking through various different hallways, you pass the luggage carousel where boxes and boxes of items are being lugged off. Somebody tells you a man was just murdered here this morning. Then he offers you a hotel. Very cheap *na*, that Tagalog accent.

Outside the airport, where you wait for a taxi, is fantastic bedlam so you light a Hong Kong brand cigarette and watch.

You take a taxi to Manila's new domestic airport which requires waiting for a pre-paid taxi while many other taxis wait with their engines off. Then you fly into Cebu City. Now 2,079.51 kilometers from her, the trash cans have all their instructions—glass, trash, newspaper—in Italian. How did the airport authority buy them? you think.

Cebu City looks like the Yucatan. It is the first place in the Philippines on which the Spanish landed, the beachhead in the cold war between Catholicism and Taoism. This rift separates the Philippines from other Asian countries. The Catholics rule.

She is a Buddhist, with a dark brown, beaded, bracelet.

The temple you visit is adorned with great big flying eaves built out of big colorful wooden dragons. It is an old Taoist temple up high in the mountain overlooking the Cebu coast. There is a sign on the wall that says *no inappropriate behavior*. This is the Philippines and you imagine that in one of the temple gardens there is an old man with a nineteen year old girl and he is sneaking off her panties.

Her friend told her that you were with another woman so she got drunk, started crying, and threw things. She knocked on the neighbor's door. A Japanese woman answered, with her man peeking from the couch. "I love Japanese," she said. She is Korean, from Busan originally—a port-city close to Japan. You know how Koreans traditionally hate the Japanese for being enslaved previously as a Japanese colony. Say "comfort woman" to a Korean and you'll get a tearful, blustery saga of why the Japanese are animals. You may even see one during fervent nationalistic protests in downtown Seoul cut off a pinky finger to show how savage the oppressors were. There's some powerful martyrdom. Liana wasn't as extreme, however, she did end up naked on the bathroom floor, somehow, vomiting beside the toilet. She had been drinking Korean Soju and eating

Doritos, and the vomit was mostly iridescent chips. You forced her into the shower although she didn't want to go.

After she was clean you lay her in bed with covers pulled up to her neck. You closed the door to the bathroom. Nobody wants to clean up orange vomit. When you opened the bathroom door the next day it was like sliding down her throat.

You come North via winding roads flanked by palm trees. There is one town that is inundated with female factory workers in blue uniforms. After three hours in the taxi, past varying towns, savannahs, bays, cliffs, we get to a town called Maya. There, You get on a rocky little boat made of wood via a wooden plank ladder with nailed on wooden steps leaning against the bow of the boat. It is hard to go up while holding a bag on one shoulder. To get to the plank you have to scale down a little mound of rocks. It is some experience just to get there. Some boys who work as boatmen offer their hands for help while shooting sardonic smiles because of their advantage in know-how.

The boat has wings that tilt down to stabilize it. It is crowded—mostly with vendors and their items. The island, Malapascua, is isolated. So they go and hawk their items.

You sit in the cramped boat under sun for nearly half an hour. Under the water there are bright blue starfish sprawled on the shallow sea-floor. Is there even a departure schedule?

You glide out propelled by a man pushing off with a long bamboo pole. There is a motor—started with a string—which is controlled with a rope connected to the throttle and a bamboo stick connected to an outboard motor. A man starts the motor after away from the shore. The boat soars on the turquoise water. After docking in the low water at the beach, you jump out the side while holding your bag slung over the shoulder.

The beach is lined with small dried palm roof huts and fishing boats parked on the shore. There are dive shops. Behind all this is a wall of palm trees. A snorkeling guide tells you four thousand people live on this island. He says there are World War II wrecks—sunken Japanese ships—right off the coast that you can see underwater. On one wreck, starfish stick to the bow.

Late in the night you take a walk with a girl with one lazy eye. She is a local and her English isn't so good, so you hardly speak to one another. She's cute and you want company. The sun sets along the beach but not over the water. You are on the wrong part of the island for that. There are many people on the beach, old men who smoke, boys playing soccer, couples leaning on the boats and watching the sun. When you stay still you see crabs scurry sideways.

She takes you inland on a small path through the lush forest. You would easily get lost if you were alone. It reminds you of the Mayan myth of Ixtabay.

There is a myth in Latin America about a woman named Ixtabay who comes out to men who have walked around a certain tree thirteen times. She is dressed in a somewhat sheer white dress, wears her long black hair straight, has penetrating eyes, and supple skin, seems to be as trustworthy as a mother yet piercingly seductive. According to the legend, if the lost man kisses her, he will die.

This story is always in your head, popping back in here and there, especially when people ask about Central America. You have thought about it and these are the possible meanings that perhaps can be culled from it:

1. If you search out depravity you will lose your way and be killed by it.
2. Beautiful women are dangerous.
3. Don't walk unknown forests alone.
4. Walk in a straight line when lost (if you have circled the same tree that many times you're sure to die).

You arrived at the airport with no ticket. Everyone else seemed so organized. Even their adventure is planned. You yearned to be different but it is of little use. What happened was you had to wait quite long because you couldn't get on any plane that would leave shortly. Rather than being unique you seemed merely disorganized.

Weeks later in an isolated island off mainland Thailand you pass a small restaurant showing an American sitcom. It is packed with foreigners, their eyes glued to the petite TV.

It is said that heaven is in the clouds but you were there, up above them, and there were only rude flight attendants who took your water without providing a new one, screaming kids, and impatient old men in conflicting plaids trying to get in the cramped bathroom before you got out.

Now below them, 1185.21 kilometers from her and on a tour in a Thai place you can barely pronounce, you find the water is about a yard deep. It's a dirty gray color. You arrive at a parking lot in front of a dock. It smells like lemon, gasoline, garbage, smoke and peanut. There are many mini-buses all filled with tourists—Westerners mostly, with a few Korean and Chinese groups. You pass some people sprawled on the ground selling small items, then get on a Thai speedboat. There is a pretty girl in a black tank top sitting alone in front of your boat. You can sit with her but instead sit with a young German and chat with an Israeli family in front of you. You race through various canals to a floating market.

You get off the speed boat, walk across the dock to the heart of the market. It is abuzz with noise, people calling out things in Thai—most ending with *kap* or *ka* depending on the sex of the speaker. It's hot with all this cooking and body heat around so you find yourself flinching when people near you. You don't like the way they walk so close to you, the Thais. Give a brother space, you think.

Pushed away from all the hubbub you pay to board a smaller, paddled boat. You now float through this crowded canal, one of a thousand bumping boats. Part of you is giddy from the clamor of people, water, boat-engines, and birds, but another part of you wants to scream and run somewhere quiet. On both sides of the canal are stores: wooden framed things built on stone. Most boats are paddled, but some have outboard engines. Comparing one boat to another is like comparing a bee to a beehive. People sell mostly useless knick-knacks that can be bought in Bangkok for cheaper. The novelty of the floating market costs you. Some boats sell fruit, some souvenirs, and a few ambitious vendors stock the boat with all those many things for making just one Thai noodle soup. The whole affair is clouded in smoke: from the boats, the idols, the shrines, the offerings, and from the various vendors who light incense.

Liana's Mayan day-sign is smoke. When you gave her a card for a birthday, before you invited her to your apartment for dinner and chased her around until she agreed to give you a kiss, you signed your name and drew her day-sign in blue felt pen—it looks like a an incense stick with smoke rising from it. This sign is for people who want to watch and see. Liana's eyes are magnificent—something like those of a cat, they shift and focus, her pupils are like the fibrous inside of an orange coated by a coffee bean, and they seek things out and see into and through them. She is pretty, but more out of a look of wonder and vibrancy because actually her face is quite large—probably to contain all that ubiquitous machinery behind her eyes. She is tall and holds her head high like a captain on a ship—like Wolf Larsen looking out from *The*

Ghost into the whiteness of white, scouring the oceans looking for *The Macedonia*, or like Darth Vader peering out at the universe from a Star Destroyer. Her body is nice but straight. She does not contain curveballs, she relies solely on the speed of her heater.

She comes from Korea which is a bit of an anomaly for a girl like her. This country of girlish male models overacting on billboards, of duos of men picking their noses at the same time in public, or screaming red-faced and soju'd in public, of woman spitting on the street and shoving you out of the way, of auto-glorified generations of farmers now in suits frying rotten vegetables in pig fat, where everything is a copy—less stylized, déclassé versions of originals from countries they insult while emulating, lacking the new ingenuity like the Japanese copies, or tradition and style of places like Thailand or Malaysia—this sameness gives her eyes nothing to study. Her country is like a game she's played too many times and mastered already. The outcomes that unfold before her never surprise her. It's a place she dearly loves—it's her home for god's sake!—but that she must go beyond if she minds the deeper part of her feelings, irrelevant of parents and boyfriend.

Sometimes people called her "The General" because of her power to make strategies, or they called her "UN" or "Kofi" which was the English nickname she chose during college when Kofi Annan was the secretary general of the UN, which was an offshoot of her Korean name *Kyong Hee*, a transliteration. She thought Kyeong Hee and Kofi sounded almost the same. You liked to call her Ana instead, taken from Annan with the double n deleted, which, when you said it gently, made her pollinate. Then you realized how she often used people for her benefit, that was the crux of her strategy, and added Li to the top to make Liana, which really changed your perception of her and hers of herself. You inadvertently empowered her.

She started to look at jobs on the Internet because you always said you would leave Korea, where you worked for a year. She couldn't imagine life without you. You were her entire source of weekend happiness. She was the Liana, you were the host. She was tired of everything else. And when she was tired of something, she strangled it to death and kept climbing. She found Allen-Bradley by accident really, while just wondering what her options were. Soon they were in contact with her asking if she was willing to join their team in Kuala Lumpur, Malaysia where they were building a monorail through Bukit Bintang—the most expensive part of this city that rivaled any as one of the most ornate and developed of the world. Malaysia was shooting for first world status by 2020 and the Petronas Twin Towers and the monorail were going to be a key part of their success. Liana even asked you if she should go. She had to try it, you said, if she didn't she would regret it and resent you for it forever. Nice guy that you were, you couldn't live with that.

So here she was in Malaysia and she missed you and found herself worrying. You had cheated on her before and now she found she didn't completely trust you. She once had seen an angry girl bang on your door, then march in and smash your computer. Now, why wouldn't you answer the cell phone at dinner time? And when you did, why were you talking so low? When she did connect with you, it was great.

You enjoyed voice chat on MSN and often tried to get her to flash you while using a borrowed web-cam so she would make those strange faces you loved. The problem was she always had somebody around. It was like she wasn't yours anymore. She seemed more curious, you thought, and you worried what about.

You planned for her to stay with you for her two weeks off in April, but then her new friends wanted to go away with her—and you couldn't go there with them because you didn't have time off. They would go to Thailand during its peak season. You couldn't take it. You felt betrayed, like you had driven off a cliff and were merely waiting for the inevitable crash.

She promised to call, said her friends told her going to see you would have been a mistake—a waste of this incredible, possibly one-time experience and opportunity.

That's horseshit, you thought.

Still, you loved her and could stand it. Again this Steven would be with her. He was definitely sniffing around her. He was often with her when she called. She said he had a Malaysian girlfriend, but you thought to yourself: where would this alleged girlfriend be on this trip? If you asked, however, Liana would accuse you of being jealous. So the only choice was to wait and see what happened. You had always been crap at waiting. You were one fidgety fucker.

You expected her to call and, though you wouldn't admit it to yourself, were always keenly aware of where the cell phone was, and if its battery had enough life. Five days went by with nothing. That Friday you stayed out all night—jumping from club to club and downing vodkas that were yours and were picked up randomly (not out of malice just a need to imbibe all) and staying very late into the evening after the groups came together and left together and you found yourself picking up a desperate Miss Lonely-hearts at a notoriously sleazy pick-up joint. In bed, you found her quite sweet, and actually better-looking than in the bar. She really didn't have to be a Miss Lonely-hearts at all. She seemed so sweet you didn't feel you needed to use a condom. At home with the girl naked on your bed you worried then the phone would ring. You had been longing for Liana to call and now were hoping that she wouldn't. It was the first time. This was a profound change. You never spoke to the club girl again, although she called often for a week. Liana did call—using a few leftover minutes from Steven's phone card. This is what really did it. All you wanted was a few private words from her to allay the worry, but you found yourself listening to a dial tone as she hung up saying there was no money left on the card. You cried—when was the last time you cried?—face down on the bed.

Now in the very city, on the very same tour that she was on then, you ride through the market, the boats always seem to be tipping you into the putrid water. This can be to force you to stop the obsessing for your Liana.

The jungle is a race to the top; a liana is a parasite, a woody vine, that uses another tree to get to the bright layer of the rainforest at the top and flower or fruit. Sometimes it even kills the original tree and lives on its corpse, stretched out triumphantly over the canopy—getting all the sunshine it can.

There is the sound of birds and frogs, both made from a ribbed, palm held wood block with mallet the Thais sell to tourists. Each time the mallet is raked over the uneven wooden edge it makes the ribbit-tweet sound. Liana loved the sounds you always make to add oomph to a story. As the boat docks, you think you see her up ahead until a Thai teenager turns around.

In a few weeks you will dream that you are on a big speedboat racing in canals and arrive in a kind of cafeteria. On the wall you'll see your manuscripts hanging reverently.

In a few weeks you will see, in real life, one of your friend's novels in an airport bookstore. You will think it's a fluke—a pure coincidence, she is talented but not famous—until you see it again. You look closer and find that since you have left the US it has been made into a Hollywood movie with star actors.

You say, she only loves herself. That's why she met him.

Maybe, Maybe not. She says, I never want to see him again.

But you did?

Yes. I wanted to clarify things.

So you went to his place.

Yes.

You should have known what would happen.

But it shouldn't have. Adults need to talk.

You say, she knows there is no talking about this kind of thing.

I was naïve.

You say, you don't buy it!

She says, take me on the sink in the bathroom.

You're all talk!

She says, she has bouts of smuttiness. They must be satisfied. Doesn't matter who by.

You say, that's not true. You will watch her blink. You hope it isn't.

She stares at you, sizing you up.

She says, it is true. I want you to call me an ugly pig and fuck me until my pelvis breaks.

Okay, then.

No, she turns her face away and says, it's too late. The moment has passed. These things cannot be contrived.

It hasn't passed.

I don't want to talk about this anymore. Forget it.

You stare at the side of her hair. You cannot believe her actions. This is not the behavior of a woman, you say.

She says, tell me a story. Something happy.

Keith Manning was an artist from London. His friend from adolescence, Morgan, came to America during college to get an American degree, plus he had a penchant for women with a Southern drawl. Symmetrically, they often liked Morgan's accent.

Keith had been moderately successful in London but still lacked true confidence in his work. He came to visit Morgan for a couple of weeks in August.

Morgan had recently come to New York to work and had met a Northeastern girl with a three part name like Mary Jo Caruso, no, it was Lizzie Jane

Sanders. He said the name sounded Southern to him and he was engaged.

Keith asked Morgan to help him, make some calls, and get him some appointments to show his work.

Morgan Van Buren phoned a gallery in Soho and said that he had a friend who was a talented British painter and would they be interested.

They said they could, if not busy at the moment he came in, take a glance but it was unlikely. They almost never, accept work unsolicited. They said they preferred agented artists for payment reasons—this payment complication was only exacerbated by Keith coming from overseas.

When Keith arrived he asked Morgan if he had called any galleries.

"Yes," Morgan said, "they're looking for talented young London painters."

Keith took a portfolio to Soho. He gave a quick, confident pitch to a woman while she cleaned up spilled coffee. The owner enjoyed hearing his accent and his style of overemphasizing his words. Keith pointed out his own strengths. Presently, he had his work, three paintings in all, accepted for a group showing.

Tell me a story, she says. About your life before.

You played the traditional boleros. Sometimes men hired your mariachi troupe to give serenades. In the middle of the night you stood outside a maiden's window. If she loved the doting man she turned on the light. If she didn't want to marry him she left the light off. Often, mom switched on the light and the senorita rushed to shut it, or the damsel went to flick it on only to find her father's abrasive hand around her wrist. There were times the light flickered on and off as you strummed your nylon-string guitar with butterfly inlays outlined in jade.

You earned enough for college books.

She says, you're no good because you always spend all your time with another new woman. It's too bad, she says, because you are sweet, and your unmentionable part is so big and fits in so well. You make me come. But it wouldn't be fair. Us. I want someone to care about me and you don't and never will.

I could, you say. Just I can't be possessed by a woman.

That is not caring, she says. Other people care.

Other people are small-minded sheep, you say. They don't do what they feel.

You are a hypocrite, she says. You say you follow your feelings but you don't. You are too cowardly to really care for someone. You take the easy way, never allowing yourself to be vulnerable.

It is quiet under here. Still you're 997 kilometers from her, precisely at sea level as you dunk your head in the water wearing a snorkel. It's like being in a nether world. There's no sound but the sound of your own breathing. It's so strange. A large part of your world has suddenly been taken away from you. There is no sound but the sound of your own breathing. It's almost as if you no longer exist. This and death don't seem all but a hairline apart. You wonder, do other people think like this?

You are swimming to her! You are swimming to her! 997 kilometers to go!

No, you are swimming next to an island with tall limestone cliffs. It's a beautiful spot. Surely they will soon shoot a movie here then organize tours to visit, litter it up, and kill it. But that doesn't concern you now. What interests you is that these cliffs continue underwater textured with seaweed and plants and fish and giant clams. As you look further down, it continues down deeper than you can even see. Are you looking into hell, a deep, dark, silent watery hell? What a horrible way to die, to drift down there, land on a big mushroom coral, drown while seeing a steel-skinned swordfish amble by.

Maybe you are already dead, you ponder. This is it. You've been put in a fish tank. You are re-born, reincarnated as a fish.

That's crazy that kind of thinking, but this water will do it to you. Look at that! It goes down further, the cliff, and it's dark. What's under the ocean floor?

What's deeper than deep? The Earth's core? Molten lava? In the US there's a stupid axiom that if you keep digging you will reach China, but from here you'd reach the US. Somehow this terrifies you. You've gotta get back on land.

As Gao says, you say, you can tell by looking around that the owner of this room has no rules and regulations.

Who's this Gao you always talk about? A Buddhist?

A Chinese novelist, you say.

You talk about him like he was a prophet, she says.

Isn't that what writers are?

She replies, what kind of food do you want?

In the bar at night you order a bucket filled with Red Bull, Vodka, and Coke. Yes, literally a bucket: it's like five drinks in one. You feel free in the bar—

free to talk to people, to dance, to keep moving. The problem is you are sweating. Maybe you are like a shark that has to keep constantly swimming or die. Or like a hummingbird. If that stops its heart explodes. You don't know what happens to the shark if it stops. Does it just fall dead on the ocean floor? What a lonely place to die: next to a dumb pulsing mushroom.

You are always on the move now, always going somewhere, and have recovered from the anxiety. Your brain was not yours. It belonged to your company, the thoughts around you, the responsibilities of going to work, of being in a staff room, of shaving, brushing teeth, drinking water before sleep to ensure mild hangovers after heavy drinking and not enough sleep, of sending text messages, making dates, trysts, plans, of planning, organizing, manipulating, and more planning—that's the word of this century—everything that can possibly be planned; now you are just going. Like the shark.

Perhaps accountability is a corporate illusion.

You bask in this revelation. Then it fades.

This is just the talk of an obscene amount of caffeine and alcohol from this bucket-sized drink.

"Be Faithful" is playing now. Fat Man Scoop, from Brooklyn, New York all the way to Phi Phi Island, Thailand. Brooklyn will never leave the world alone no matter where you go. The beat of this song is strong, undeniable. You quickly strike up a conversation with two striking girls. Together you go to the dance floor and let the music surf through you until washing up on the shore with strong cigarettes and another bucket of that drink.

You think of the morning underwater.

You can't see the tide underwater, you say, but you can see everything react to it.

This isn't enough to start the embrace. You are old enough to know it's time to go to bed and sleep.

You call Liana from the hotel and say, you want to see her.

Come visit then, she says. She misses you.

This weekend?

She's free, she says. Friday's a holiday. Come then.

I'll call you tomorrow and confirm. I have five more days before work.

The next day, you book your ticket. Then you dial Liana's number and when she answers, blurt out: I will come tomorrow!

Didn't you get my email, she says.

No, why?

Her parents are coming. They are surprising her for the long weekend.

You are back in Bangkok airport, merely a 743.27 kilometer flight from her: a puddle jump. Your ticket is still for Kuala Lumpur but any self-respecting person would go home. You, though, have these romantic notions that if you show up with flowers, even if her parents are there, it will be magical. However, you also sense that even though she said parents it is probably something, or even someone, else.

You are sitting in the domestic wing, reading, or trying to read. Your eyes follow words but the meaning floats and drifts like an invisible tide.

You have bought a statue of Buddha with one hand gesturing in a temperate 'stop' motion. You believe in this kind of thinking all of a sudden, after years of 'go hard' thinking. This Buddha doesn't have the Christian *be righteous* message, it's a 'go', but not hard, just 'go' as you will. Slowly, quickly, whatever. It's not exactly a gesture of 'stop', but more a gesture of 'stop hurrying'.

There is a Chinese restaurant next to a neat rectangle of chairs riveted to the floor. A large column to hold the roof lintel divides the waiting room seats. Behind the seats is a currency exchange with an ATM machine. Many tourists of different sizes and colors of skin with backpacks and luggage piles wait in their seats. They wear the expressions of waiting—blankness, the opposite of curious. You marvel at them. If someone looks at you, that person will find you gawking.

There are seats that are vacant on the left of the column. It's strange that so many people are shoehorned into the seats to the right of the column and so much emptiness remains on the left. There must be some mistake. The universe must be laughing.

There is a sign beside the column but you cannot read what it says. You get up to read clearly in black letters:

This Section is Reserved for Monks Only.

You write her a postcard. On the front is a temple with flying eaves and big colorful dragons. You have written a loving message to her. You want devotion and love—and stability. The problem is everything is moving. The only way to achieve this stasis is to go, to move, to roll.

You understand this when swimming, or bucket-deep in vodka and Red Bull, but in a few days when once again buttoning up your button-down shirt you will not remember. Peace is fleeting. This is no secret. The recollection vanishes. How to get to that peace dissolves. The imprints of where you have been in your mind and in your life stay but unfortunately the footprints of how you got there disappear, leaving you disjointed and incomplete. This kind of thinking, the kind that is interested in and maintains the footprints but not the destination is what matters, but this kind of thinking is not for your kind.

You go to the thick, orange, airport phone, insert your credit card, and dial. You lean your hand up against the glass while you hear the foreign tone pulse.

No more calls, she says.

But we need to talk, you say.

Talking is for fools!

Then we are two fucking morons, you say.

It cannot go on like this, she says. It's always the same pattern.

You don't want to hear it, you say. Now you know you're tired of it.

I am going to smash this phone, she says.

Don't! You rest your head against the partition glass. Talking is our last hope.

It's hopeless then, she says. She hangs up.

You dial again.

It rings a long time. Then there's that energy in your ear when the receiver connects: a vast vacuum of space and possibility.

I said no more calls, she says.

She wears a Buddhist bracelet on her wrist and smashes her phone with the ball of her foot.

Just come get me when you want, she says. But you will never hear it. You stare at the flying eaves on the postcard. After staring for about an hour you are left with the image of her in a floral—or was that paisley?—dress. You stand and smile. You walk to the ticketing counter. The agent smiles at you.

Then you sit down in the empty monk-reserved section.

A police officer bows politely and says, sorry, sir, you're going to have to move. This section is for monks only.

###

Ralph-Michael Chiaia writes fiction and poetry. He has a book called *Ten Poems & Ampersands* about life travelling Asia. He also has another book about the Maya and life in Latin America called *Glyphic*. He has short fiction called *For Monks Only* that is his version of Soul Mountain.

Ralph was born in Staten Island, New York in 1975. He grew up in Montclair, NJ. When he lived in Mexico and Guatemala he was struck in the gut by the Sacred Calendar. He has since resided in Asia. At the time of writing this book he was living in Seoul, South Korea with his wife and son. Still he considers Montclair, NJ and Long Island, NY his home(s).

Check him out at ralphmchiaia.com. If you put in your email at his site you will get a free book of your choice.

If you want to see more rambling musings, check out Ralph at his blog ralphadelic.blogspot.com.

Please leave a review

If you enjoyed this book, please leave a positive review where you purchased it. Authors need a little bit of praise and social proof to make sales so we can make more books you enjoy reading.

Other Titles by Ralph-Michael Chiaia

Ten Poems about East Asia
& Kitsch Nebula Ampersands And

Glyphic

The Sacred Calendar

Praise for Glyphic (a novella in verse)

"An urgent and prophetic poem about the violence of big business on the soul."

—Cecelia Chapman, writer/artist

"I am not usually a fan of poetry, but these were well written and easily decipherable."

—Rachel Collings

"Chiaia's verse is lightning fast, clear and unencumbered, but the story can be murky and tangled, not sure if it wants to be an encomium for an ancient people, a philosophical treatise on the nature of time, an exposé of the Guatemalan genocide, or just a swaggering, self-absorbed adventure.

A wild trip that gets lost--but it wants to."

—Kirkus Review